WITHDRAWN FOR SALE

This edition first published in 2018 by Gecko Press
PO Box 9335, Wellington 6141, New Zealand
info@geckopress.com

Reprinted 2018

English-language edition © Gecko Press Ltd 2018
Translation © Sally-Ann Spencer 2018

Text & illustrations: Antje Damm

Title of the original edition *Der Besuch*
© 2015 Moritz Verlag, Frankfurt am Main

English-language edition arranged through
Mundt Agency, Düsseldorf

The translation of this book was supported by a grant
from the Goethe-Institut, which is funded by the German
Ministry of Foreign Affairs.

GOETHE
INSTITUT

Edited by Penelope Todd

Design and typesetting by Spencer Levine

Printed in China by Everbest Printing Co Ltd, an
accredited ISO 14001 & FSC certified printer

ISBN hardback: 978-1-776571-88-8
ISBN paperback: 978-1-776571-89-5

For more curiously good books, visit geckopress.com

The Visitor

Antje Damm

Translated by Sally-Ann Spencer

GECKO PRESS

Elise was scared of everything.
She was scared of spiders,
scared of people
and even scared of trees.

So she never went out.
Night or day.

Elise liked her house to be neat
and tidy, so she cleaned it every morning.
Sometimes she opened a window,
to let in fresh air.
Then one day something
unbelievable happened.

A strange thing flew
in through the window
and landed at her feet.

Elise looked at it.

"That'll have to go!" she decided.
She scooped it into the fire.

But that night…

she was too scared to sleep.

The next morning she heard knocking.
No one ever knocked at her door.
Why would they?
She certainly wouldn't answer it.
But the knocking didn't stop.

In the end she opened
the door. She stared.

"I'm here for my plane," said the boy.
"Umm…"
"And can I visit your bathroom? It's urgent!" he added.
What shall I do? wondered Elise.

Then she heard herself say:
"The bathroom is upstairs on the left."
The boy climbed the stairs and disappeared.

It seemed like forever.
And then he came back.

"Who's that?" he asked.
Elise looked at the picture.
He waited patiently.
"It's me—when I was young,"
she said with a little smile.
"I was invited to a dance and
I wore my prettiest dress."
"Cool!" said the boy and he looked
around some more.

"Have you read them all?" he asked.
"I have!" said Elise. "Every single one."
"Will you read one to me?"

It was a long time since
Elise had read to anyone.

The boy wanted to hear
every story in the book.

Then he wanted to play.

When he got hungry,
Elise buttered him a
slice of bread.
"I think you should
probably go home
now," she said.

That sounded a bit sad.

"What's your name?" asked the boy.

"I'm Elise," said Elise. "And you?"

"Emil," said the boy.

"Bye, Elise. It's fun at your house."
He waved goodbye.
"Bye for now, Emil," she said.

When it grew dark that night, Elise
knew exactly what she wanted to do.